This book belongs to

Lara

Bath New York Singapore Hong Kong Cologne Delhi Melbourne

Narrator	Cindy Robinson
Young Tiana	Elizabeth M. Dampier
Young Charlotte	Breanna Brooks
Tiana's Father (James)	Terrence Howard
Tiana's Mother (Eudora)	Oprah Winfrey
Tiana	Anika Noni Rose
Prince Naveen	Bruno Campos
The Shadow Man	Keith David
Mama Odie	Jenifer Lewis
Ray	Jim Cummings
Louis	Micheal-Leon Wooley
Big Daddy LaBouff	John Goodman
Charlotte	Jennifer Cody

Produced by Ted Kryczko and Jeff Sheridan
Adapted by Cherico
Additional music created by Gannin Arnold

℗ 2010 Walt Disney Records © Disney Enterprises inc.
Unauthorized duplication and use prohibited.

This is a Parragon book
This edition published by Parragon in 2010
Parragon
Queen Street House
4 Queen Street
Bath, BA1 1HE, UK

ISBN 978-1-4075-9577-1
Manufactured in China

This is the story of "THE PRINCESS AND THE FROG".
You can read along with me in your book. You will know it is
time to turn the page when you hear this sound.
Let's begin now:

Once upon a time, but not so very long ago, in the southern city of New Orleans a little girl named Tiana was visiting her friend Charlotte LaBouff. Charlotte lived in a lovely mansion. Tiana's mother was there too, working on sewing a dress and telling the girls a story at the same time. In the story, a frog was really a prince who was cursed and he needed a kiss to make him human again.

Tiana frowned. "There is no way in this whole wide world I would ever, ever, ever – I mean never – kiss a frog. Yuck!"

But Charlotte smiled. "Is that so? I would do it. I would kiss a frog. I would kiss a hundred frogs if I could marry a prince and be a princess."

When they returned to their own home, Tiana helped her father finish cooking dinner. They dreamed of someday opening their own restaurant. Soon the whole neighbourhood gathered on the front porch to share the delicious gumbo they had made.

Later, as her parents tucked Tiana into bed, she pointed out of her window. "Daddy, look! Charlotte's fairy tale book said, if you make a wish on the Evening Star, it is sure to come true."

Her father nodded. "Yes, you wish and you dream with all your little heart. But you remember, Tiana that, that old star can only take you part of the way. You've got to help it along with some hard work of your own and... and then, yeah, you can do anything you set your mind to. Just promise your daddy one thing. That you'll never, ever lose sight of what's really important, okay?"

After her parent's left, Tiana made a wish to the Evening Star. "Please, please, please."

As the years went by, Tiana became a beautiful woman. Her father had passed away and she worked waiting tables at a placed called Duke's Diner. But Tiana still dreamed of having her own restaurant so she worked very hard and saved as much money as she could.

In another part of the city, a prince from a foreign land walked down the gang plank of a ship. Prince Naveen was not a hard worker at all. His valet, Lawrence, carried all of the prince's luggage. The prince was visiting New Orleans because he loved jazz music and the city's famous Mardi Gras festival was starting which would be filled with great jazz music.

All the people in town were excited by the prince's arrival. Everyone that is, except Tiana. The festival was a busy time for her work and she also cooked on the side, so that is where she focused her energy.

Later that day, Charlotte LaBouff and her father came into the diner. She told Tiana that Prince Naveen was coming to her father's Mardi Gras masquerade that night. "I'm going to need about five hundred of your man-catching beignets for my ball tonight." That big order finally gave Tiana enough money for the down payment on her own restaurant.

PRINCE ARRIVES TODAY

Naveen

CHE
50 I
W

To Be Held

Prince Naveen of Maldonia
WORLDS MOST
BLE BACHELOR

Soon after that, Tiana made an offer to buy the old sugar mill. She and her father had chosen it as the best location for the restaurant a long time ago. With her mother by her side, Tiana imagined how it would look when 'Tiana's Place' was finished. "Just look at it, mama! The maitre d' is gonna be right where your standing. Oh, and over here, a gourmet kitchen. I gotta make sure all daddy's hard work means something."

Her mother frowned. "Tiana, your daddy may not have gotten the place he always wanted, but he had something better. He had love. And that's all I want for you, sweetheart."

At the same time, in another part of town, Prince Naveen and his valet, Lawrence, were having their Tarot Cards read by a man known as the shadow man. He promised both of them he could give them anything they wanted. Lawrence wanted to live like the prince, not just work for him, and Naveen wanted to avoid princely duties and keep his carefree lifestyle. The shadow man showed them a magic talisman. Soon Lawrence transformed to look like the prince and the prince was turned into a care-free frog! The shadow man had used evil magic to make the switch.

That evening, Charlotte was thrilled when the prince arrived at the masquerade ball. She didn't know that it was now really Lawrence in disguise. She happily danced with the impostor. The shadow man planned to have Lawrence marry Charlotte and then they would steal all of her father's money.

Across the room, Tiana was serving her beignets. The men who were selling the sugar mill were guests at the ball but they gave Tiana bad news.

"You were outbid." If she couldn't come up with more money, Tiana would lose her chance to buy the sugar mill. She was so upset she tripped and fell onto the table of beignets. Her costume was ruined.

Seeing her friend's fall, Charlotte rushed Tiana upstairs and gave her a beautiful blue dress and princess costume to wear. Then Charlotte hurried back to the ball. Alone, Tiana walked out on the balcony and looked up. She saw the Evening Star and closed her eyes to wish for the sugar mill.

She opened her eyes and saw a frog. To her amazement, the frog spoke, "Kissing would be nice, yes!" Tiana shrieked and ran back into Charlotte's room and the frog followed her. "I am Prince Naveen of Maldonia." He explained he had been cursed and needed a kiss to become human again. "Surely I could offer you some type of reward. A wish I could grant, perhaps?"

Tiana wanted to help him and thought getting her restaurant could be a perfect reward so she closed her eyes and kissed him. There was a flash and she looked at Naveen. He was still a frog. Then she looked in a mirror and screamed. "What did you do to me?" Tiana was a frog now, too!

The shadow man had planned on keeping his frog prince a captive but Naveen had escaped. But he needed to keep Naveen close to make the magic talisman work and keep Lawrence looking like Naveen.

The two new frogs were chased out of the mansion, out into the bayou. There Naveen learned that Tiana wasn't a real princess. "Well, no wonder the kiss did not work. You lied to me!"

"I never said I was a princess."

"You never said that you were a waitress. You were wearing a crown."

"It was a costume party, you spoiled little rich boy!" Then Tiana learned that Naveen didn't have money to help with the restaurant. His parents had cut him off from any more money until he learned to be more responsible. But right now their bigger problem was how to get out of the swamp.

In the morning, while Naveen still slept, Tiana built a small raft. Then as she struggled to paddle them through the bayou, Naveen lazily strummed a home-made ukulele. So far, she was doing all the work.

Suddenly an alligator popped up next to them! "Uh, oh." But he wasn't hungry. He was a jazz lover. His name was Louis and he loved playing the trumpet. He came by because he heard Naveen's music. Naveen and Louis seemed content just to talk and play music but Tiana wanted to find a way to break the spell. Louis told them about an old voodoo woman named Mama Odie who lived in the bayou. He thought she might be able to help with such things.

Meanwhile, back at the estate, Lawrence was proposing to Charlotte. Without the real Naveen nearby, the talisman's magic was wearing off and Lawrence was slowly changing back to himself. But Charlotte was so excited about becoming a princess, that she didn't notice. "We're going to have ourselves a Mardi Gras wedding!"

Off in the bayou, Tiana and Naveen were learning that being
frogs wasn't easy. They tried to catch a firefly with their sticky
tongues but got tied up in knots instead. The firefly kindly helped
them untangle. "Let me shine a little light on the situation." Then he
offered to lead them to Mama Odie. The firefly's name was Ray. As
he travelled along with his new friends he told them of his true love.
He said her name was Evangeline. "She the most prettiest firefly ever
did glow."

Naveen advised him. "Do not settle down so quickly, my friend."

Tiana was getting tired of the 'all-play and no-work' prince. She worked faster to hack through the bayou and find Mama Odie.

Suddenly Naveen was scooped into a small net. Three hunters wanted frog legs for dinner. Ray raced in to help. "A bug got to do what a bug got to do." He flew right up the nose of a hunter.

But the other hunters netted Tiana. Working together the two frogs hopped out and about causing the hunters to hit each other as they tried to get them. Soon all three men lay battered at the bottom of their boat. Tiana called out. "And we talk, too!" The shocked hunters fled in fear.

After all that excitement, everyone was hungry. Tiana started to prepare a swamp gumbo for dinner. Naveen wanted to help, but he didn't know what to do. "The day my parents cut me off, suddenly I realized I don't know how to do anything."

Tiana began to see the prince in a new light. She taught him how to chop mushrooms and they made a gumbo. Ray and Louis loved what the two frogs had cooked together.

When they had all finished eating, Ray pointed up at the sky. "There she is – the sweetest firefly in all creation." Everyone looked up expecting to see his true love, Evangeline, but it was really the Evening Star. Louis began to play his trumpet and Naveen asked Tiana to dance.

But a few minutes later, powerful shadows sent by the shadow man swept over the bayou and grabbed Naveen. As they began to drag him away his friends tried to pull him back, but the shadows were too strong.

Suddenly flashes of light vaporized the evil shadows. Naveen was saved, but how? "Not bad for a hundred ninety-seven year old blind lady." It was Mama Odie!

The magical woman and her pet snake led the four friends into her shrimp-boat home.

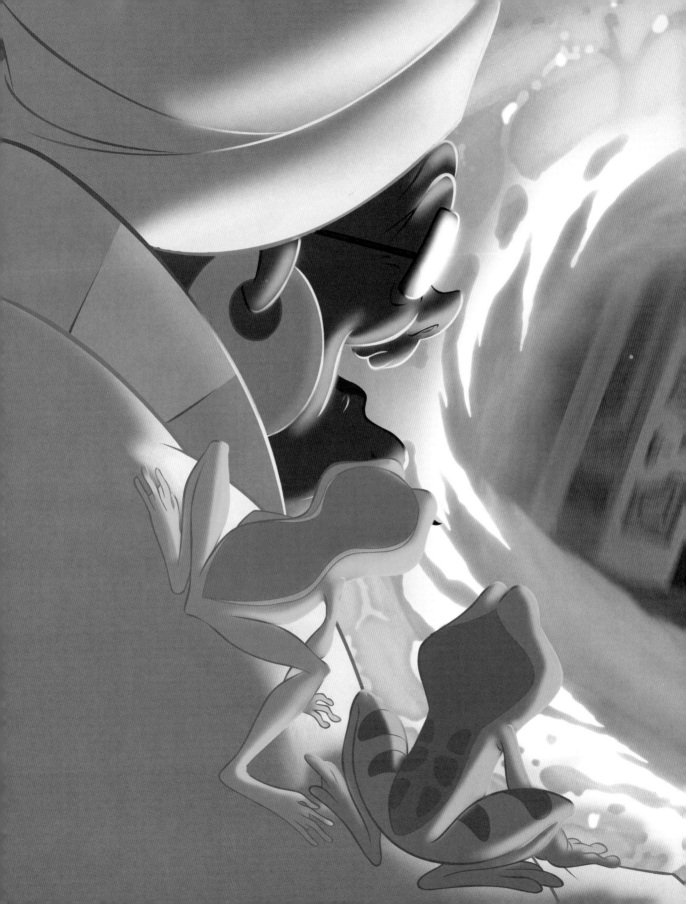

Mama Odie knew why the frogs were there. "Y'all want to be human but you're blind to what you need." The frogs didn't understand. The old woman sighed and began to stir her gumbo. "Gumbo, gumbo in the pot, we need a princess, what you got?!"

Tiana peeked into the tub and saw a vision of Charlotte becoming the princess of the Mardi Gras for the night. Mama Odie told them that if Naveen could kiss the 'Princess of the Mardi Gras' before midnight, they could become human again.

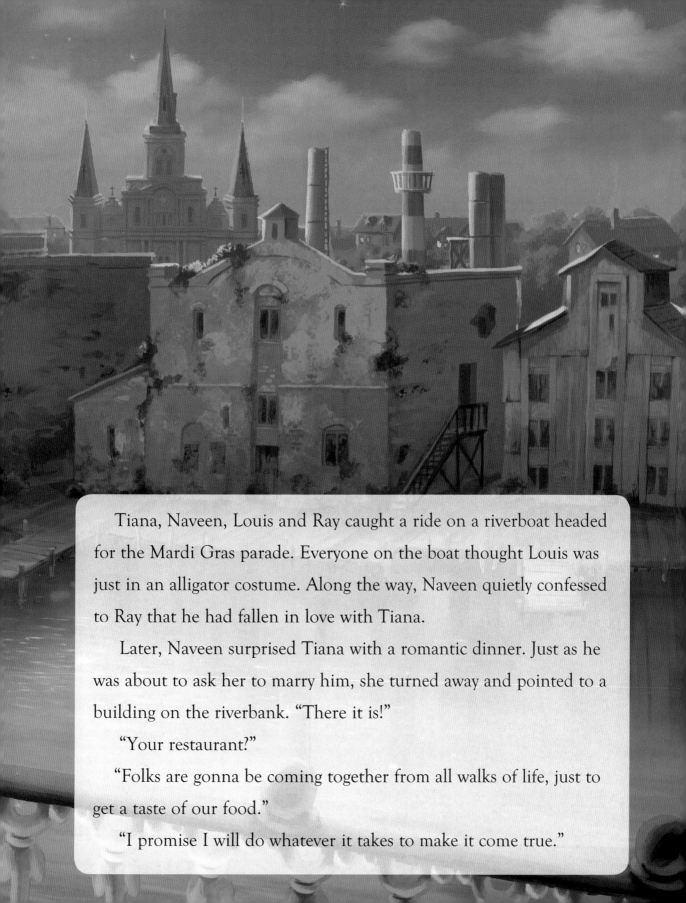

Tiana, Naveen, Louis and Ray caught a ride on a riverboat headed for the Mardi Gras parade. Everyone on the boat thought Louis was just in an alligator costume. Along the way, Naveen quietly confessed to Ray that he had fallen in love with Tiana.

Later, Naveen surprised Tiana with a romantic dinner. Just as he was about to ask her to marry him, she turned away and pointed to a building on the riverbank. "There it is!"

"Your restaurant?"

"Folks are gonna be coming together from all walks of life, just to get a taste of our food."

"I promise I will do whatever it takes to make it come true."

Naveen hopped away. He knew he could not afford to help Tiana buy the sugar mill, unless he married Charlotte.

As he sat alone on the deck wondering what to do, the evil shadows swept in and captured him! They quickly delivered Naveen to the LaBouff estate where Lawrence and the shadow man were waiting. The shadow man used the prince to restore the talisman's magic. Soon Lawrence looked like the prince again. Only now did Naveen fully understand their wicked plot, but they locked him in a chest.

Meanwhile the riverboat landed and Ray accidentally told Tiana
how Naveen felt.

Tiana was thrilled and they raced to the parade to see if Naveen had
kissed Charlotte yet. Instead they saw Charlotte and a human Prince
Naveen getting married! Not knowing that it was Lawrence in his magic
disguise, Tiana sadly hopped away alone. Now she thought she would
be a frog forever.

But Ray suspected foul play. He found the real Naveen and released
him from the chest. Together the two friends arrived at the wedding
float just before the couple said 'I do'. Naveen grabbed the talisman
from the impostor's neck and flipped it to Ray who sped away. The
wedding was stopped!

In a different section of the parade, Louis was having a wonderful time, living his dream and playing his trumpet in a Mardi Gras band. Then Ray flew by with the talisman, which was heavy for a firefly. The shadow man and his shadows were in hot pursuit and gaining on him. Louis leapt off the bandwagon and followed the action to help his friend.

Then an angry shadow man caught up to Ray and swatted him to the ground before continuing after Tiana.

As his shadows closed in, the shadow man blew a puff of magic dust over Tiana. It created the illusion that she was human again and in her dream restaurant. The evil man smiled. "All you got to do to make this a reality is hand over that little ol' talisman of mine."

At that moment, Tiana understood everything. Her father had been surrounded by love. He always had what he needed and had never forgotten what was important. So Tiana smashed the talisman on the floor. "No! No!"

Immediately, Tiana was back to reality and a frog again. But the shadow man had lost control over the evil shadows. "Do you have any idea what you've done?" The shadows chattered and swirled around him. Soon all that was left of the shadow man was his black top hat.

Tiana hopped off to find Naveen.

She found the prince with Charlotte, the Mardi Gras princess, along what had been the parade route. Tiana arrived just in time to hear him agree to marry Charlotte. But he added a condition. "You must give Tiana all the money she requires for her restaurant. Because, Tiana, she is my Evangeline."

Tiana called out. "Wait! My dream wouldn't be complete without you in it."

Tears filled Charlotte's eyes. "All my life I read about true love in fairy tales, and, Tiana, you found it!" She turned to Naveen. "I'll kiss him, for you, honey. No marriage required." But the clock began to chime. It was midnight and the kisses came too late.

Tiana and Naveen were still frogs but they were together.

Suddenly, Louis ran up to them carrying Ray. The firefly's light was flickering low. The swat from the shadow man had hurt him badly.

Tiana and Naveen stood by him, held their hands together and told their friend all that had happened. "We're staying frogs, Ray."

"And we're staying together."

Ray smiled. "I like that very much. Evangeline like that, too." And then the little bug's light went out for the last time.

Later, in the bayou, it was time to bid Ray good-bye. Ray's friends raised their eyes to the Evening Star. Next to it there was another bright star no one had ever seen before. It seemed Ray and Evangeline were together at last. The little firefly had been right all along. True love always finds a way...

Not very long after that, as all of their friends watched, Tiana and Naveen were married by Mama Odie. As the ceremony ended and the two frogs kissed, they turned back into humans!

Mama Odie laughed. "Like I told y'all, kissing a princess breaks the spell!" Once Tiana had become Naveen's wife, that had made her a princess.

Tiana and Naveen then went back to New Orleans. Their parents were happy to see them safe and hear all their good news.

A few months later, there was a new restaurant in town called, not 'Tiana's Place' but 'Tiana's Palace'. Tiana and Naveen enjoyed working there together and Louis played music and sang with the band. It quickly became well-known for great food, exciting music and good times.

Tiana had everything she'd ever wanted. Sometimes dreams and wishes can come true.